I0788441

WORD

A COLLECTION OF POEMS CIRCA 2003-2023

Jerica Floyd

Bluebird Publising

Contents

Introduction

 **Thank you for embarking on a soul-stirring odyssey with me through ink and verse. I'm an author who fearlessly delves into the depths of the human experience. From tender moments to raw emotions, my poetry weaves tales that provoke thought and touch hearts. Join me on this transformative journey as I share my evolution from a wide-eyed seventeen-year-old to a seasoned writer at the ripe age of thirty-eight. Together, let's explore the power of words and embark on an unforgettable literary adventure.**

-Jerica Floyd

Responsibilities - 2003

I said I was going to be your girl

Right after running my 17 year old cousin

to the hospital, cause she's giving birth

And remind me to pick up flowers at the gift shop

for my best friend who got shot yesterday

And I promise

Right after I sign this petition to save

little black boys from becoming victims to this

machinated system

I'll be your girl

But first

I gotta save revolution from being trapped inside

white pages and black ink

And of course we can go out on a date

But not on Monday

Because that's my feminist day

And I'm too much of an independent woman

to have some boy paying for my lunch

So, we'll have to schedule this date somewhere between

The sanity of my imagination

and the insanity of my reality

So that'll be either Wednesday or Friday

Not Thursday, because at some point I need

to become black super woman

and save all my black kings from being nigga peasants

and all my black queens from being unpaid prostitutes

Because everybody knows that everything but change

comes to you when you're buying societies stereotypes

As a matter of fact

Lets cross out Wednesday

Cause on Wednesdays I freestyle

For all those that don't have 5 dollars

to hear me spit at a coffee house

I'll be free styling words out of alphabetical order

So you can understand bullshit even when it's scrambled

Taking my rhymes to the stage for your ears to listen without regret

Cause this piece of knowledge won't cost you

the lottery ticket you'll never win on

I freestyle just so you know that the revolution

comes with no prepaid advantages

So I guess that leaves Friday

And you know what

That's actually my relax day

Where I contemplate on the weeks events

and sit pretending to meditate to myself

In all honesty

I'm to busy to become any boys, girl

See, I have to

Defend my blackness to all the dark skin sistas in the morning

Pretend to be white to all my teachers

Come home and trap poetry between the walls of

truth and authenticity

Hoping that conformity and commercialization don't bulldoze through

I haven't made appointments as a girl since 1996

So you're going to have to reevaluate yourself

Put some complexity to your motor skills

Quit telling me to be your girl

cause we're a long way from playing kick ball at recess

You need to

Politely, court me as your woman

That is

If you're ready to be a man

Cause I can't make time for maybe

I need certainty

A man with strength enough to

cry because his feelings for me are too overwhelming to process

A man with so much understanding of his woman

that he answers questions before the words leave my lips

A man with so much sensuality and depth of his woman

that a kiss on the neck could make

my mental, spiritual and physical bodies

Orgasm

Simultaneously

Can you handle that?

Cause I'm ready to be your woman

And if you can be a man

Then

My calendar is clear

Personification - 2003

This poem is strong
Realizing that the world wants to dehumanize it
Waiting to cut up the only meaning of life it has
Criticizing the words that make it
Saying, real poetry is fantasy
And this is just bullshit

This poem is truth, cause no one told me
That friends are deceiving
Multiple personalities and I'm the one that's trippin'?
Family members find facades to show in public
While entertaining private thoughts of your destruction

This poem is not naïve
So no,
Don't bring me your pimped up lines of
Baby girl, I just want to be your man
Trying to find your way up the sweetness of these thighs
Cause, this poem knows that the last thing it needs
Is to push out 7lbs and 3 ounces of responsibility

This poem knows that it can never be a full adult
Because the little girl lost inside still needs to be a daddies girl
But adults never want to admit they're wrong to a 17 year old
And a drunken father can never see the real meaning
in the hurt of his daughters words

This poem has been a feminist

Activist, communist, socialist, revolutionary
And sometimes, a stereotype
Who realizes
That poems aren't the only ones
That can stand on their own two feet

Haiku - 2004

I
Black, it was deep, free

I dived into it head first

Ain't came up for air

II
Love, Misunderstood

Physically I was taken

Mentally, I lost

III
I thought freedom was

He, you, she, I, us, them, they

Someone lied to me

Poetry - 2004

The world had a lock on my lungs
Somewhat like the restriction they put on my words
Only this felt like two hands clutched around my throat
Allowing air to seep through only when I gave up my pursuit
Of finding myself
These hands started to squeeze tighter
Until,

I found him

In the backset of my mother's Camry
When the wind no longer blew in my face
but, danced across my cheeks, softly caressing my cheeks
Whispering verses of fantasy in my ear
He became pure oxygen to me
And I
So tired of having my air restricted
Inhaled

I found him

Caught in his understanding
His words were keeping me sane
As I watched my generation dive deeper into insanity
He is truth
I discovered in the abundance of my soul
Spoken through my pen caressing the pages in my mind

I was lost in the freedom he shared with me
And I realized those hands clutching my throat were conformity
A silent killer wanting me to be like everyone else
Wanting me to stop struggling and wear the personality
they assigned to me
A system trying to force me into their definition of normal

I found him

Sitting next to my cousin in a pew
Finding that I can use him to talk to the Lord
Write my prayers in haiku and limericks
I confess my sins in 5, 7, 5 format
And he answers

He found me

In the suppressed thoughts of my childhood
Through the tip of a pen
I was waiting

We found each other

When I was searching for a friend
Looking for truth
He appeared
Dressed in Nikki Giovanni and Maya Angelou garb
I walked into the world with him
Taking my first real breath

It Always Falls On Deaf Ears - 2004

I was tryna force myself not to write

Everyone wants to hear

But no one wants to listen

My words are becoming obsolete in this idealistic society

Where anything I write is looked at as only ink on paper

Easily replaced by red, yellow or blue

But always with that white background

Trying to force me to be anything but left

In this right handed world

Continuing to reach into my pocket

Pulling out my identity

I was losing myself in truth

Forgetting its definition

Making me realize that

I never knew what it meant in the first place

Truthfully, I'm more obsessed with the thought of it

Cause I've been fed nothing but lies throughout my life

Why give you the pleasure of eating a chocolate soufflé

When all I've been given is this American pie

Shoved down my throat

Containing acceptance of this machinated government

Presidents with criminal records

And no sir, I will not support this country

Because it's been over 400 years and you've yet to support me

But, of course you're not listening

Cause what sense does it make to

care about what your people are saying

I reject your conformity

Not because I'm different

But because I was never one to accept society's emptiness

You fail to see me because you don't realize

You're viewing me with closed eyes

Seeing the label your social imagination has provided you with

I'm not a stereotype

So don't confuse that bulge in my belly for another bastard baby

To be brought up in the slums you've provided us with

Broken beer bottles along the curb side

Pimped up suits worn by too many female abusers

Local pedophiles hanging on the steps of elementary schools

While you drive by in my college education

And yes, I include racism in every one of my thoughts

'Cause no one else will

All I have is this poem

It's the only way you'll let me talk

I've figured out that

By my skin color, I should know nothing

And by my gender, I should be maudlin

But by these words, I'm going to be angry

'Cause you refuse to understand

Won't even open your eyes enough to

See how drastically the streets are evolving

Brothas putting on iced out crosses and throw back jerseys

Tryna live out that dream of making it to the NBA

Fake thugs caught up in hip-hops mistakes

Niggas saggin' their pants below the waist

Showing how ready they are to be some mans' bitch in jail

Chasing low self esteem in a short skirt

Talkin' bout how fine they be

How many pennies they have to make up that dime piece

Not realizing that a hand full of change

can never make up common sense

Television has been showing them false identities of black youth

So they think hustling is the only alternative

The music industry has you treating

Young ladies like video hoes

My pen is tired of writing about the same problems

And receiving no solutions

So you can clap, stand up or snap those fingers

Pretending you're hearing me

Or thinking that you've heard this somewhere before

And you're probably right

But the redundancy is necessary

Because, at what point

In the reading of this poem

Did you actually start listening?

AAMU PC - 2005

I was sitting at open mic
Thinking how open the mic would be
to me speaking into its electricity
Hoping a little of its power could flow into me
Cause, I'm starting to get inspired by
Messed up relationships and
I'm drowning in his soul love poems
I was hearing poetry of praise for
fellow African sisters
So, I took out my pen and said, damn

I want to write some hot shit!

Some, get out yo seats
this is the black revolution 50 years' early type shit
Some, I write because words free me
from society's emptiness
And things never happen if you don't plan
So, this poem is my map and the pen is my compass, type shit

I wanna write something hot!

Some verse powerful enough to
turn hoes into housewives and thugs into understanding
Some, there are good black men out there
We just need to stop treating them like dogs
Then get mad when they start performing tricks, type shit

Some verses about a paranoid schizophrenics' thoughts
Cause I think the government be following me
Somehow, they know when I say fuck America

Damn!

I wanna write
And write ain't even the right word
Cause right things never fall apart
But everything that writes me
seems to wrong conformity
And have these so-called politicians
trying to burn the poems in me

I was getting inspired
to write of broken streets
and broken neighborhoods
That keep children trapped in its walls of
Low income and high rent
Your words poured on me struggling families
Where no one plays the adult roll
Leaving little girls to guess what the definition of woman is

The flow was picking up
Poems started racing through my pulse
Like murder thoughts run through a psychopaths' head
I plot to kill illiterate black boys and girls mentals of
Wanting to be bad bitches and thugs

I write societies wrongs on pages of contracts
Signed by my pen that was burned in hell
then saved in heaven
Give me inspiration, Lord
I'm trying to baptize this crowd

with prose and limerick
I want to write something hot
And create this continuous flow
Of me feeding off you and you feeding off me
Occasionally serving main courses to homeless
minds starved for knowledge

If I have successfully accomplished my mission
You should go home dreaming about this
Wake up thinking about this
Take out that pen and book of poems and say

Damn!
I wanna write some hot shit!

Killing Time - 2005

I was sitting on the porch scribing one day

Tryna to kill time

When I realized

Time is usually killing me

It has me living by his rules

And his restrictions

I need my independence from him

I need to rewrite the emancipation proclamation

And free myself from him

Cause he has me living on a 24 hour schedule

And my body runs at a 32 hour pace

So

I figured I could gather all my clocks and dump them

Taking that

Out of sight, out of mind approach

But I guess that only works with divorced parents and their children

So

I'll recycle it

Cause maybe then I can keep recycled minutes and seconds
at my bedside

To re-up whenever I'm running low

But of course, that won't work

Because

How can you recycle what you can't touch

So, now

I'm trying to treat time like those cash loans

Told him

I'll give you ten minutes tomorrow

If you would just spot me five today

And of course I was denied

Cause I don't live in the correct proximity of good credit

Then

I decided to just breakup with him

Cause this relationship is not working

And it's not you

I said

It's me

But time is possessive

Aggressive, even

Laughs at my breakup notes

And slows time during my 9 to 5

He may be delusional, but we are over

You know,

I had an epiphany

Time is more of a personal possession when you have money

And I've always been broke

So

My final answer

My final solution

Is taking time and holding it for ransom

I don't know who'll pay the bill

But somebody better give me ten million minutes
in unmarked seconds

And while you're at it

Take 3,504,000 hours of free labor that you received from us

During those 400 years of slavery

Multiply it by $37.50 and pay it in full, America

I am through asking

I am telling

I'm on a rampage

Time can no longer conquer me!

I speak it loudly and without fear

Because I mean to destroy it

I'll take over all time zones

And we'll live in leisure

With no restrictions

Endless breaks

Timeless frolics on the beach

Unmeasured naps and gameplay

2 second workdays and 80 hour weekends

Father time will be slain

Obituary read live on CNBC

Death to all punchcards!

It Is What It Is - 2006

So, they say that

Every one has had their heart broken

Their mind cheapened

Their mental thought process clouded by

Hard dick and soft lips

I understand that all poets aren't sincere

Or even truthful for that matter

Looks like Ima have to start dating Bic, ball point pens

Since they're the only ones that are real

And yes, I personified pens

And I'll probably personify paper so I can have a man on the side

Cause these humans ain't all they cracked up to be

And I'm not bitter

I'm just understanding

Finally

I know that a kiss don't mean I'm yours

And that sex doesn't mean we're exclusive

But, damn

It would be nice if life were that simple.

12 Steps - 2006

So he said I couldn't be his 'cause I was too radical

Guess he got mad when he offered me

That penny for my thoughts

And I said that's not even market value

Infinite price plus your soul is what I'm asking

There will be no other offers on the table

This is non-negotiable

Either you have it or you don't

And he obviously didn't

So for two quick seconds

Ima step out of my radical voice

To talk about everyday bullshit

Why I gotta dress like a ho to attract you

Be a freak but not too freaky to keep you

Be a woman with intelligence around your family

And a maid waiting on you hand and foot around your friends

Pretend to not understand so as to feed to your ego

And all the other steps of your 12 step program for

Women who are too radical

Well this is a poem for every brotha out there who claims to

Want an enlightened sista

Then gets scared when she starts to speak her mind outside of a poem

This is the 12 step program

For niggas disguised as men who don't know what the hell they want

And it starts off with consideration

That means, when you say 'I'll call you back'

Actually pick up the phone and call back

Next Ima need you not to refer to me as Mrs. Beaver

'Cause there will be no cooking breakfast, lunch and dinner

Until you realize that I do it out of love and not duty

Step three will be you picking sides, either you want to be

Aware vibing with Marley or

Ignorant two stepping to pedophiles and fake gangstas

Four, if you want to be a man, you're going to have to look the part

'Cause those sagging pants, oversized shirts and hats

Will not do

And just know

Brother in the making

That I am not trying to transform you into a yuppie

But little fish become dinner unless they pretend to be sharks

Try and understand my reasoning

Step five is changing your vernacular

From European to African

And greet me as your queen

Steps six and seven

Will involve you taming that little boy inside

Who keeps wanting to jump out and play these games

Who refuses to carry adult conversations and

Can't decipher the difference between thinking with his brain

And thinking with his head

This will aid to you when entering grown folk relationships

Step eight will be detox

Three weeks without those lame excuses

Without those kindergarten lies

And I was at my boys house for 7 hours bullshit

Steps nine, ten and eleven will fuse your mind body and soul into one

So you can love a woman physically, mentally, and sensually simultaneously

Step twelve will be you conquering your fears

Getting over that afraid of commitment bug

Understanding yourself enough before jumping into the complexities of a woman

And last will be you disregarding this poem

Because a real man knows that becoming one

Comes from introspection of self

And no 12 step poem can teach that.

Loss - 2010

I think I'll be able to write again
When the words don't taste so
Bitter on my tongue

Reality has found its way into my heart
And has left no room for old loves

Who let me sculpt them
Into solid pieces that
Look a lot like truth
Where I breathe my soul inside
To give them life
And that
Is the reason why
They danced across my lips
As if they were mine, and mine alone

But I haven't seen them dance in a while

Not since my stumble into this realm
Where truth is more than a
Well dressed politician with a
Devilish grin and reassuring handshake
Or a girl gone lost
Who thinks a rub on the butt is
The same as a caress of the heart

It's having to tell your mother that
You don't blame her at all for the

Life you left behind
And smiling when she has to shave her
head for the second time

It's being the rock for others to
Break themselves against
When all you want
is to be broken

It's watching some stranger pump
Glowing liquids into the same arm
That held you at night when you swore
That dragons were in your closet.

It's telling her that,
This too shall pass
And you have to spit out
Every word individually because
The taste of the lie is so strong and potent
You don't want it to seep into your heart

It's trusting God even when he threatens
To take away what secures you

It's realizing that it was she
From whom I took the clay
To mold my truth
Her who gave me poetry
My words

It's hoping that she gets to see
My children grow
And wishing that if this is not a possibility
That she leaves me a bit of poetry
To write of her beauty for everyday she is gone.

I think I'll be able to write again
When the words don't taste so
Bitter on my tongue

Wishful Dreaming - 2012

If I'm conscious enough

Between that sliver of time

When asleep and awake

I run

As fast as light

To the top of the highest mountain

Sword in hand

Demanding

He send you back to me

Power - 2013

All hail the New World

Where order is set

by the same color of the earth you walk on

so we must be grounded

From her we sprouted

Bright as the Son with inevitable quickness

and

A sharp steeled tongue with political slickness

Which pushes through doubt and stabs through fear

What say you?

Be we peasants or be we royalty?

Rhetorical

Your eyes should hurt at the brightness of your reflection

Who say I'm not as tall as a red wood

easy going like a stream and deep as an ocean?

Who say I'm not fly enough to dance on Venus

Use the stars as my necklace and swim through the milky way

Who say you not?

Who say you not Queen like We

or

King like He

Your eyes should hurt from the brightness.

I claim this

That's why I

spit fire like a volcanic eruption

my truth so profound

it takes no assumptions

I am where the world is

my womb is what birth it

so that gives me

power to burn it

power to change it

rearrange status quo

And put Caucasians in cages

revolution is mine

I put my name on that blacklist

I'll change the whole world

with a flick of my pen

and I dare 'em to stop it!

Verbs and Nouns - 2013

Seeing, knowing, believing, reaching

hoping, loving, being

Being

This ing

that forces movement

That suggest you do instead of theorize

This ing that creates me

Coruscant

I glow so bright

I think the Son is my father

Perhaps I'm gasconading

But only because

I wrote poems in the trails of my mothers amniotic fluid

to be birthed through the gene-ius of those words

That formed me

Stretched my legs and let out a cry

That broke into a million pieces

which pushed through the universe

sprouting worlds of consciousness and truth

But truthfully, I lye on the daily

straightening twisted mentalities that rock

A. Davis hair and reality show brain

Where naturals seek the callipygian ideal

And I keep wondering where all the Queens went

Ladies being first and all...

A Most Definite Problem - 2013

I have a problem

I wake up humming a delightful tune

and this is new to me

because I'm not a morning person

I'm more of a

Growl, coffee, sigh, coffee person

And stranger still

When I open my mouth,

I sing

And though I have no business singing

I do

and sometimes I do a little dance

Which I should never do

but I can't help myself because

I met you.

and before I met you

There were no morning tunes

No dancing

No singing

But now...

Now there's you

And there's music

and I have a problem

I don't want to stop singing.

Kanye - 2014

I know better

I know that situations change things

I know that the absence of a butterfly

gives birth to chaos

I know that Kanye could've been Kendrick

Had his butterfly not died

I know that boys live in their mothers womb

Long after they've been birthed

I know that death is more than loss

It's a mark

The invisible stamp that lets you

in that club of grief

Where minutes are as long as you need them to be

I know that wounds heal

I know anything coming back to life

hurts like a thousand knives to the body

I know that we are resiliant

We cut our teeth with diamonds

and learned to walk on active volcanos

I know that we are Gods

I know that man seeks to

destroy all that is more powerful than him

I know thats why rainforest die

I know that 1 plus 1 equals 2

Except in case where women are involved

and 1 plus 1 can sometimes be 3

I know that we are magic

We create this world by

stretching our bodies beyond contortionist limits

I know what Joy is

I know it sounds like a babies first breath

and feels like a little kick to the ribs

I know better

I know that little boys are

birthed from their mothers wombs

But never from their hearts

I know that losing your tether to this world

Can cause you to be lost in this world

But we come back

I know that we can come back

A Conversation of Awesomeness - 2014

He got closer to my head

Is that...

Is that glitter in your hair?

And I gave him a look that made him immediately explain himself

Because it's sparkling, he said

No disrespect it's just, I don't usually see hair that...sparkles

And I said

It's not glitter

It's the galaxy

He smirked, you're playing me, right?

It's cool sister, he said, I meant no disrespect

But it is...I say

The galaxy

My coiled strands are built from stars

The very start of life lay in these strands

Aquarius, Virgo, Cassiopeia all reside in these strands

And when I stretch them straight

and watch them pop back in place

those stars scatter about the room giving life

to those searching and the truth to those listening

So it's glitter, he says

Weren't you listening baby, I say

It's the stars

Step a bit closer and you can get

pulled in a black hole by these

coily constellations

He stepped closer

I smiled, it's glitter, I say

Nah, he says, lips pressed against my ear

They're stars.

Common Sense - 2015

There was a time when

I thought he wanted to leave

But then I realized

No one could eat my pussy that good and want to leave.

Hey Black Woman - 2015

Hey Black Woman

Why you so perfect?

Seeing you thrive makes me blush

I get shy and awkward

I get speechless, then

Stumble over my words trying to find the right ones

Tripping over stereotypes

Trying not to become one

Why you so fly?

How you sip tea with Jupiter

and roller skate with Saturn

Can I come?

I'd hang out with Pluto

Just to prove I'm not trying to

use you to meet stars

I'm trying to learn why you glow so bright

and why can't they see it

I see gold laying under that epidermis

Sparkling when the sun hits

Cocao brown, caramel twist

Deep dark coffee shades to the ones melanin barely kissed

I see shine in every hue and it fills my soul

Makes me proud to be brown

Makes me want to

have 10 little girls and

watch them be proud to be brown

Hey Black Woman

Why you so Queen?

Coconut Oil - 2016

Ima pour nothing but coconut oil over my life

Ima listen to Erykah Badu and get my soul right

Ima vibe to Jill Scott and find that sensuality again

Nothing but movies with black actors, black directors, black writers

Ima get that culture back

Ima swim all in that culture

let my skin soak it up like the sun

Get golden brown, tanned type blackness

Ima let these curls get kinkier

Ima quiet these doubts

Ima assassinate the insecurities

Let the God in me shine through

She gone be proud

She gone glow bright

She gone scare those fake friends away

They'll gossip around empty bottles of wine

wondering why their skin takes on a green hue when I'm around

She gone correct my posture

and make me stand tall in front of these oppressors

Ima get our kingdom back

Ima give them 40 acres

and take everything else

Ima be free

Ima have a pride of children

And they'll be free

Ima turn Scars into Mufasa's

And they'll be free

Ima return the crown to black women

And they'll be free

Ima keep pushin

Ima be fearless

Ima be ruthless

Ima be Queen

Ima be all my ancestors

Im a warrior

I wont fail

All Lives Matter - 2017

We were niggers

Monkeys, coons, spooks, niggettes

It was out in the open

Real knew real and

Fake knew fake

It wasn't harmonious

But it was a raw truth

There were clear lines and nowhere to hide

Then we were Negroes

Sophisticated

Occasionally Colored

And we were dignified

The Negroe in America

The educated Negroe

The good Negroe

The fair Negroe

The watch your step, look down and don't challenge us Negroe

Then we were African American

Now we were apart of the country

Now we were what they were

Now we were real

So we swept those names under the rug and we became civilized

But someone, someone reached under that rug

dusted those names off and put them in the

"Quiet as kept" room

The private conversations between family room

The, that Jamal sure can throw but no he can't date my daughter room

And we all pretended those rooms didn't exist

Those of us who did were called paranoid

Because, this is a color blind society, right?

Right?

There's no race anymore, we're all equal

What racists remarks, you do all eat chicken? don't you?

You know who your father is, wow?!

I thought it was mostly single parent homes

You graduated college, good for you! What an achievement.

The first in your family?

And suddenly things that shouldn't have been forgotten were

Suddenly it was, they're the racist ones with their black history month and affirmative action

Their black president and welfare phones

We're the minority

We're being pushed out of our country

Black Lives Matters?

No!

All Lives Matter

All lives with blond hair matter

All lives with blue eyes matter

All lives that get a fair day in court matter

All lives that are peacefully arrested after killing a church full of saints, matter

All lives that open carry weapons without being sieged upon, matter

All lives that change lanes without signaling and don't end up dead, matter

All lives that try to make a living selling loose cigarettes and get to walk away with a warning matter

All lives that shoot up theaters and live to see their day in court, matter

All lives that burn down churches and are never looked for, matter

All lives that put on blinders, misdirect the conversation because they feel uncomfortable, matter.

All lives that would defend a flag before they would defend a person of color' right to live, matter

Nigga - 2018

Ima say nigga as long as I want

how I calls my kin ain't none of yo business

when it was important, you didn't care

when it came with a lynchin' rope, you didn't care

when it came with a subservient stance, you didn't care

when it came with mass homicide, you didn't care

but now that it comes out the mouth

of a Marcy project billionaire, it's an issue

It's disgusting, inappropriate

Do you know what that word did to your people?

now that it comes out the mouths of comics who say,

that's my nigga, you care

You care now 'cause we use it so freely

Now that we can respond, fuck you, when YOU say it, you care

Yeah, It has a history

We got some things to work out, yeah

Some demons to put away, of course

A discourse about how that word travelled galaxies

from a white mouth to mean, you piece of shit

To a black mouth to mean, my brother

Shit's fucked up

That's what happens when generations are

molested by white racist bullshit

You start acting it out, trying to work through the trauma

We know

Maybe it's a bit a self hate left in that word

A reminder that we were and will always

Be something else in this country, to this country

And we remind them of their ancestors hate every time they hear it

It's family business, we'll handle it around big momma's table

But until then, my guy is my nigga that's my brotha

And if after 500 years of slavery, mass murder and deconstruction of our family core

At the hands of your ancestors

The only thing you have to contend with is the inability to use the word, nigger, nigga

You got off easy.

Love Is - 2018

Love is

wide

open

truthful

extravagant

Over the top

In and out of time

Incomprehensible yet very understanding

Love is

Fighting for 2 hours and making up for 4

Love is holding strong through growing pains

And knowing change is inevitable

As is forgiveness

Love is knowing what imperfection is

And calling it perfect

Whispering sweet nothings and

Yelling absolute something

Love is real

and live

and vibrant

Safe and

comfortable

And full of unknowing

You will fight

and you will scream

You cry

and laugh

and hope

And wish

And there will be sorrow

There will be sadness

There will be pain

But within that

you find this light

Created by the two of you

That glow brighter than an early morning sun

And within it's warmth you know that you can battle

Anything

Get through anything

Jump every hurdle

Swim through countless oceans

And climb the highest mountains

Because

Love is

You

Fuck You - 2019

Fuck you!

It stung when I said it right?

Felt my tongue pierce through your soul hot and sharp

Did your body get tense

Did your shoulders go back

Check out your feet

Are they squared up prepared for a fight

Your body

Is on the defensive

It senses danger and is preparing for another attack.

That is what racism was like

Before it was hidden

Black people carried this defensive stance with them everywhere

Because in the eyes of their white counterparts

They could see those 2 words

And if they got close enough

They could hear those 2 words

Whether spoken or not its presence was clear

In the way they were avoided

In the way they were refused service

and in the way they had to drink from separate fountains

and in the way they were beaten

and in the way their leaders were shot

and in the way their grandparents were hung

and in the way their children were dragged for looking at pretty white girls

and in the way they were blasted with fire hoses

and in the way they were denied progression

and the way they were belittled

and in the way they were given poor education

and in the way they were profiled

and the the way they were held back

and the way they were called nigger

and in the way they were guided into criminality and then punished for it

They could hear that Fuck You loud and clear.

But today

Today that fuck you is hidden

Today, you're taught it doesn't exist

Today they give you proof that it is gone

Like having a black president

Or clubs that play majority hip hop and r&b.

Or shows with black actors

And prestigious schools with black students

They hid it and

So we dropped that defensive stance

We're not prepared for the blow and we don't expect it

But then

Something like Trayvon happens,

Something like Mike Brown happens,

Something like Eric Garner happens,

Something like Sandra Bland happens,

And there it is...

Fuck you.

I Am Allowed - 2019

I'm allowed to cultivate my own image

I'm allowed to cover my canvas in

black paint when I want to drown my past

I'm allowed to do fast, short strokes of red when I want more passion

and

slow, smooth lines of blue when I need that calm

I'm allowed to flick specks of gold so the world don't forget how bright I shine

And I'm allowed to wash it all away

as many times as I want

As many times as it takes

Until I feel that the world sees me

and more importantly

until I see me

because

I am allowed to cultivate my own image

Reassurance - 2019

I asked him if it's forever type thing

He said

Not only is it a forever type thing

Its an infinite type thing

Expansion and contraction of the universe type thing

To the stars and beyond, I'll be on my Toy Story type thing

Follow you anywhere

Become Superman, Turn back time just to start it from the beginning again type thing

This is an us type thing

I said, so it's a love type thing

He said, fuck love this is an enamored type thing

An obsessed stalker type thing

I know where every freckle on your body is

and I'll trace them to find your ecstasy type thing

This is a truth type thing

Yes you look fat in those jeans

but I don't give a fuck cause I'm in love with you're soul type thing

You tend to be long winded but I'd listen to you for hours type thing

This is a real type thing

You get to working that neck and snappin those fingers

I get to raising my voice and stomping my feet

but those are growing pains, baby

I'll always come back to you

This is a together type thing

You and I wage wars on jealous single people who think we spend too much time together

Fuck them

This is a Best Friend type thing

Passing notes at work, signing for your eyes only

This is a childish type thing

I don't want to get mixed up in the confusion of adult feelings

I want to love you like a child loves their first crush

This is an innocent type thing

Check yes or maybe because I'm too much of a punk to put no

this is a scary type thing

So, eternity I said

Till the stars fall down, he said.

Reminisce - 2019

Sometimes

I see glimpses of her

That girl I used to be

Wish she'd stay around

She made me smile

Becoming - 2019

And I looked in the mirror

So pleased with my soul

That I began to glow

Brightly

My Reason - 2019

I love him so much that

My lips

Smack at the mere mention of him

That

His soul forces its' way through the crevices of my brain

So, it can slip poetic sonnets of passion out my finger tips

I love him so much that

My lungs never have enough air to

Reveal all there is to love about him

He, keeps me enlightened so much that

Whenever he talks

I spell out our love in an unknown tongue

I-Am-In-Love with this man

And he knows

Because, every time my mouth opens

It is to speak his name

So that I can taste his aura dripping from my lips

He is King

That sit on throne of peasant worship

African spirits singing of revolution in his veins

Playing djembe drums on his heart

I love him because

He refuses to let me stand, as he sits

Offering me his throne

It grows every time he

Takes my brown sugar coated hand into his

When thunder storms interrupt our sunshine

And every time his fingers trace the outline of my curves

I sing melodic songs of his sensual IQ

And whenever he opens his mouth to express disagreement

I melt at the vocabulary of his verbs playing with nouns

Having intercourse inside well-structured sentences

And I eagerly forgive him

He colors me in such sensual tents

More than any other artist I've had

He knows how to use his brush

On the blank canvas that is me

Paints his desires in

Deep sex toned reds

Dark emotionally stroked blues

Ancestral slave ridden blacks

Sun scorched African sand browns

And bright intense yellow that keep me

Swinging in his rhythmic breeze

I am He

And he is…

He is…

Love,

Undiluted

Unedited

Prehistoric

He is…

The innocence of love

The first time it was ever spoken unto man love

The playground, black top lollipop love

He is…

Truth.

I love him because

He is my quiet on noise filled days

My man, mmmph

I-Am-In-Love

He…Is…My, reason.

Stay Mad - 2019

11,263 days it took to love the, Who I Am

Wasted time being clay for foreign

Fraudulent hands to mold me

Let them spit those lies

And asked me to drink

Like it was the polyjuice potion to

Becoming them

I contend

Fight off definitions thrown at me

Put who they wanted me to be

On tips of arrows

Then shot them through my heart

Like poison, it coursed through my veins

Locking the, Who I Am away as it flowed through

I conquer

Tossed out expectations and set them ablaze

Used the ashes to bathe in

And came out a phoenix

I scorched bone for a new me to grow

Let her correct my posture and stride

So, they know Queen when they see Queen

30 years, 10 months, 2 days, 12 hours and 43 minutes

To become the, Who I Am

And y'all can stay mad

Black Bird - 2022

Black bird singing in the dead of night
Black bird singing in the dead of night
Black bird singing in the dead of night

Black bird
Black bird
Black bird
Black boy
Black boy singing in the dead of night

Hands up don't shoot

Black boy singing in the dead of night
Just selling cigarettes to feed my family

Black boy singing in the dead of night
All I have are skittles and a juice

Black boy singing in the dead of night
It's a toy gun

Black boy singing in the dead of night
I'm just going for a run

Black boy singing in the dead of night
I can't breathe

Black boy singing in the dead of night

Is my sister...

Black boy singing in the dead of night
Mom, Mom, Mom...

Take these broken wings and learn to fly

I have Three Brothers - 2023

I have three brothers

That older one a philosopher

See's worlds within worlds

Outward and within

Has a heart two times too big

Loves hard

and

Loyals harder

Fights battles for the sake of me

For the sake of them

Fails and tries

Then

Fails and tries harder

Should have name him Socrates

An unexamined life is not worth living

and he examines it

Adjust and examines it again

It's all a process

He taught me patience

I have three brothers

That middle one a beast

King of the jungle in a tailored suit

Mathematical genius

See's what you add up to before you know the equation

He's a force

Pushes through struggle with ease

Won't let the stress wear on his face

Holds his family on his shoulders like it's light weight

Keep my burdens and secrets like it's light weight

Should have named him perseverance

It's not if, it's when

It's not how, it's how not

A thousand against him and he'll say, add a thousand more

Effortlessly

He taught me strength

I have three brothers

That baby one is light

Shines like a thousand suns

Charismatic giver of warmth

Adversity builds him, fights through negativity with barely a blink

Graceful

Loves on the rough parts of you to bring shine to those beaten parts

A restorer

Should have named him Helios

Impossible to dim his light

You only end up shading yourself

He taught me friendship

I have three brothers

Just So - 2023

I'm all straight lines and precise corners

White walls that are bare

I'm exact

Nothing out of place

Not a hair or a pillow or curtain

Or laugh

Or attitude

I am gracious and understanding

Ready to help

Yes, of course

Sure, I don't mind

I would love to

I would love to

And I generally do

Except

When, I would love to becomes

I have to

And they always do because

I'm invisible without it

Text aren't read

DMs aren't returned

I'm not invited

I'm not considered

Unless the,

I would love to's are there

I'm nonchalant

I am rubber and you are glue

I do not indulge in gossip about me

I keep my lines straight

And my corners precise

I don't ask to be included

because

That comes with a price

And sometimes I can't bring myself to say

I would love to

Sometimes those words taste poisonous

Like a betrayal to myself

So potent that I have to spit them out

And I do

Because I'm invisible without them

What is it about me that people refuse to love

Or

Include?

I keep my lines straight

And my corners precise

What's My Muthafucking Name - 2023

My name is Jerica

Associates and a few friends

call me that

My mom called me, Lucy

Her best friend called me LuLu

A few dozen cousins call me Jer

And a few more call me Jeri

My Dad calls me JeriJ

And despite the some 20 years that have passed

There's a special person who gave birth to

the most special person

and she calls me Jacob

I have a very good friend that sometimes

Calls me Jerae

And while I don't dislike my middle name

I do flinch when it's said out loud

This friend also coined me BlueJay

A name that initiated me into a poetic family

One so special that

No matter how many months, years, decades

May pass us by without speaking

I still

And always

Refer to them as family

It's funny

What we call each other

The labels we place on each other

And more

What we answer to

There was a time when I would answer to

A plethora of titles

All of them in fact

I had missing pieces

And those pieces wanted to be loved

To connect

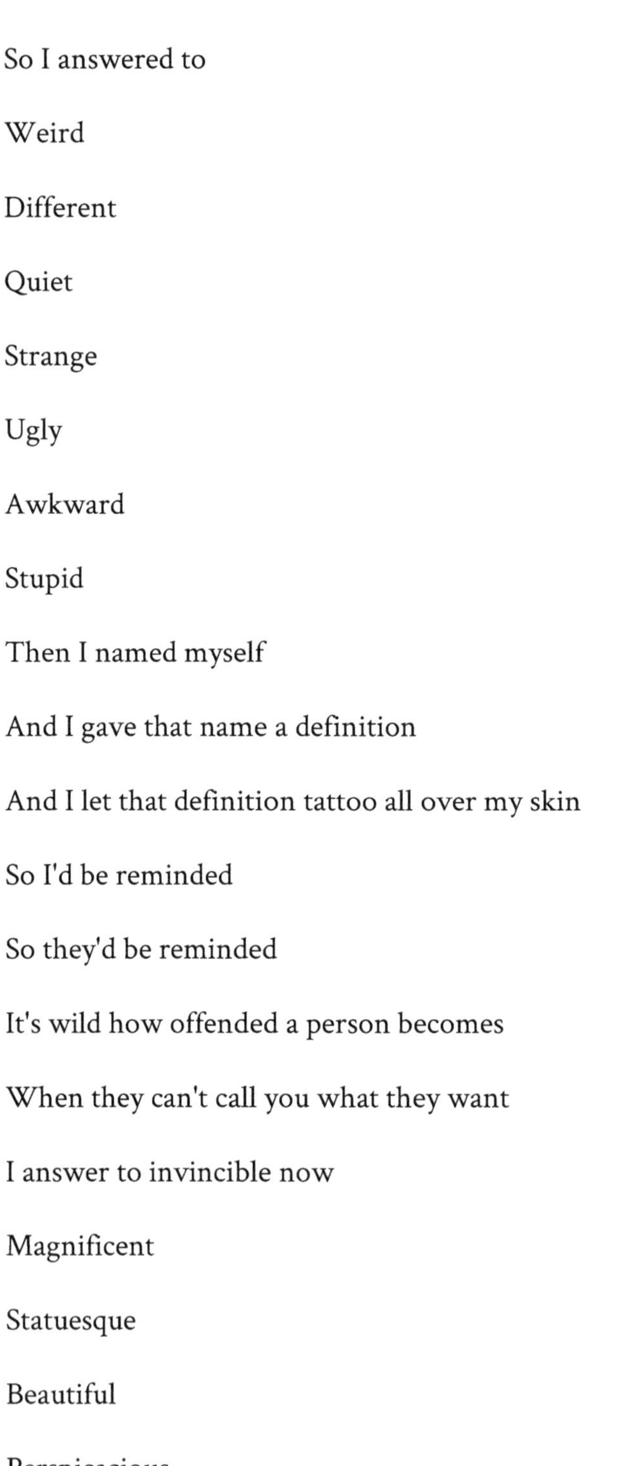

So I answered to

Weird

Different

Quiet

Strange

Ugly

Awkward

Stupid

Then I named myself

And I gave that name a definition

And I let that definition tattoo all over my skin

So I'd be reminded

So they'd be reminded

It's wild how offended a person becomes

When they can't call you what they want

I answer to invincible now

Magnificent

Statuesque

Beautiful

Perspicacious

Unprecedented

Uncontainable

Unconquerable

Unlimited

Unequalled

Undiminished

Unstoppable

Unfukwitable

Queen to all she surveys

You may know me

But you do not know my name

And therefor

Cannot call out for me

I AM

www.ingramcontent.com/pod-product-compliance
Lightning Source LLC
Chambersburg PA
CBHW041732300726
48981CB00006B/327